For Arthur, who has loved several pill bugs to death,
and for my parents' backyard in Minneapolis,
which has seen just so many funerals. —S. V. W. L.

Dedicated to Lizard. His name was as simple as his life. 2004-2016 —G. E.

STERLING CHILDREN'S BOOKS
New York

An Imprint of Sterling Publishing Co., Inc.
1166 Avenue of the Americas
New York, NY 10036

ISBN 978-1-4549-3211-6

Distributed in Canada by Sterling Publishing Co., Inc.
c/o Canadian Manda Group, 664 Annette Street
Toronto, Ontario M6S 2C8, Canada
Distributed in the United Kingdom by GMC Distribution Services
Castle Place, 166 High Street, Lewes, East Sussex BN7 1XU, England
Distributed in Australia by NewSouth Books
University of New South Wales, Sydney, NSW 2052, Australia

For information about custom editions, special sales, and premium and corporate purchases, please
contact Sterling Special Sales at 800-805-5489 or specialsales@sterlingpublishing.com.

Manufactured in China

Lot #:
2 4 6 8 10 9 7 5 3 1
06/19

sterlingpublishing.com

Cover and interior design by Irene Vandervoort

THE END OF
SOMETHING
WONDERFUL

a practical guide to a
BACKYARD FUNERAL

by STEPHANIE V.W. LUCIANOVIC
illustrated by GEORGE ERMOS

STERLING CHILDREN'S BOOKS
New York

FIRST you need something dead, meaning
something that was once alive but isn't any longer.

Your Something Dead will most likely be something
wonderful you loved very much as a pet, like a guinea
pig or a fish.

Perhaps a pill bug.

If your Something Dead didn't leave instructions,
it is safe to assume they will be okay with
whatever kind of backyard funeral you plan.

Because even dead, they know how much you
miss them, and how much you want to be able to
explain that to everyone.

But that sort of explaining can be hard. Having
a backyard funeral helps when you can't find all
the words.

(Or when they get stuck on their way out.)

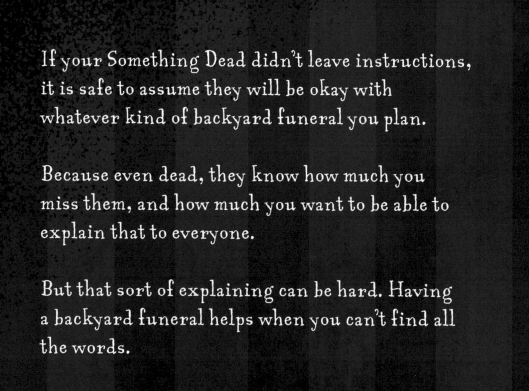

To start, it is good to put your Something Dead in a box.
Pretty much any old box will do, but avoid:

LITTER BOXES:

pee-yew — too stinky!

JACK-IN-THE-BOXES: too springy.

BREAD BOXES:

too crumby.

A SHOE BOX is usually the best choice of all.

If you want to add things to the box to keep your Something Dead company, that would be fine.

A GUINEA PIG might like an orange nub of carrot.

A FISH might appreciate a few drops of water.

A PILL BUG might be grateful for a smooth rock,
cool in your hand.

You will also need a hole.

Having lived full but small lives, a guinea pig, fish, or bug generally won't need a large hole.

Now, if you have a funeral for something really big,
like a hippopotamus or a narwhal, you will have to
get permission from the city to dig a very deep hole.

A WARNING: *Don't get excited and try bury something
that isn't dead. Not only is it rude, but it is also annoying
when the Something Dead walks away before the backyard
funeral is even over.*

Being of nautical origins, a fish might
appreciate burial at sea.

If there's no sea nearby,
the toilet is just as nice.

It is considered respectful to salute
and say something in fish language
as you flush.

(Roughly translated,
"*Blorg blub glug*" means:
"We commit fish body to the deep.")

You will want to tell stories about your Something Dead at your backyard funeral.

You can talk about what they did and how lovely they were and how sad you are thinking about all the things you shared together.

AN EXAMPLE: *"Here lies Bugward Z. Wamperjawed. He enjoyed long walks on the sidewalk, crawling up blades of grass, and avoiding birds. His life's ambition was to travel all the way to the other side of the garden. He was a good bug, and I will miss seeing him on the screen door."*

You could also explain how being dead won't ever change how much you love them. But if you don't feel like saying it out loud, it's perfectly okay to hug that thought inside your heart, too.

Funerals almost always involve the singing of songs.

Some songs can make you cry, which people do at funerals.
Some songs can make you laugh, which people also do at funerals.
Sometimes people laugh *and* cry at funerals because that can happen, too.

Even without songs.

If you do cry at your backyard funeral, have tissues handy. They are almost always better for wiping tears and a runny nose than a sleeve.

A PROMISE: *Crying because of how much you loved your Something Wonderful before it became Something Dead is not bad or embarrassing at a backyard funeral or at any other time. In fact, crying can often make you feel a little bit better. Even if it might not seem like it at the time.*

When your Something Dead is in the box and when the stories have been told and the songs sung and the tears cried, you can cover up the hole and bring on the flowers.

(No one knows why flowers are good at funerals other than almost everyone enjoys flowers at some point in their life, so they would probably enjoy them afterward, too.)

Don't dig up your Something Dead "just to see how things are going" like Mabel across the street did that one time, because when something is dead, it isn't going anywhere. Anything Dead prefers in all cases to be left peacefully alone.

A FACT: *R.I.P.* on tombstones actually means "Rest in Peace." If you were supposed to dig up Something Dead, the tombstones would say "Rest Until Someone Wants To See How Things Are Going," and *R.U.S.W.T.S.H.T.A.G.* really doesn't fit as nicely.

It's hard to know how to end a backyard funeral because even when it's all over, it might feel like it isn't.

And maybe it isn't.

You see, it's possible you still aren't all-the-way ready to say goodbye to your Something Wonderful that is now your Something Dead.

Maybe you want to curl up close to where you buried your Something Dead and have chats every so often.

Maybe you want to read them your new library book on mummies or tell them about the third grader who threw up in the drinking fountain and clogged it.

Maybe you just want to sit with your Something Dead and be quiet for awhile.

Whatever you want to do is just fine.

Funerals come at the end of something wonderful.

Just remember: it's not the end of everything.

You can always begin SOMETHING WONDERFUL again.

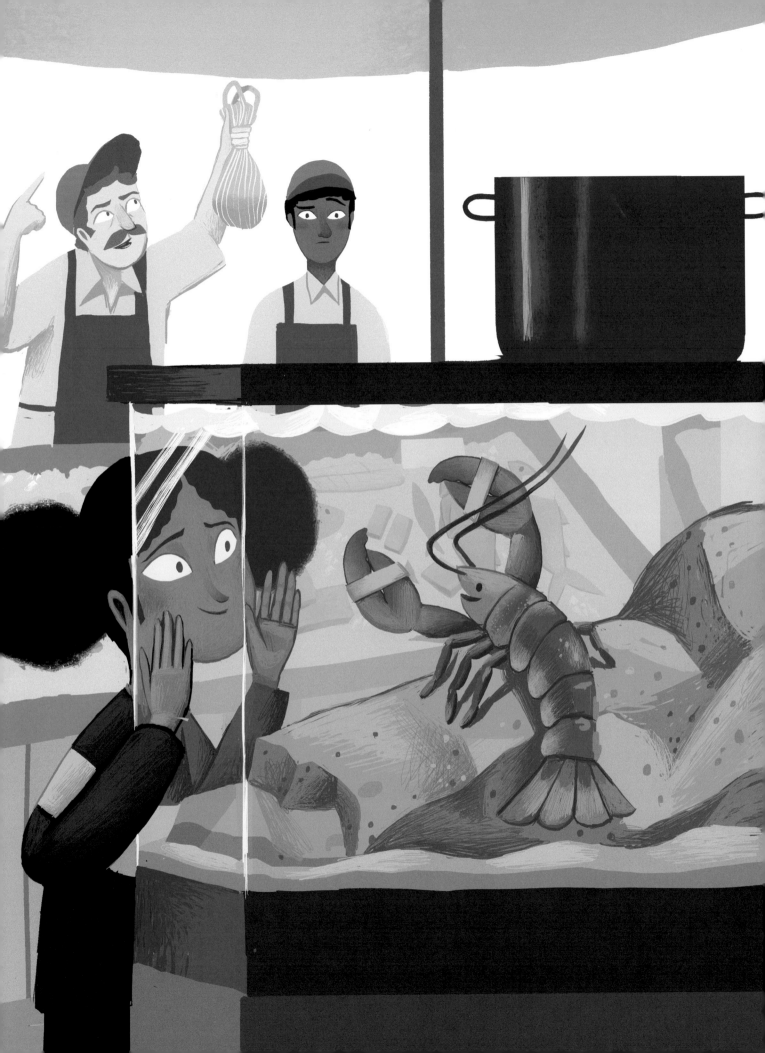